Alexander Evans

Aeneas

A Classical and Heroic Poem

Alexander Evans

Aeneas
A Classical and Heroic Poem

ISBN/EAN: 9783337193843

Printed in Europe, USA, Canada, Australia, Japan

Cover: Foto ©Andreas Hilbeck / pixelio.de

More available books at **www.hansebooks.com**

ÆNEAS

A CLASSICAL AND HEROIC POEM,

BY

ALEXANDER EVANS
(PERCY FENTON).

DEDICATED

TO THE MEMORY OF

GEORGE DENNISON PRENTICE,

THE DISTINGUISHED

POET AND JOURNALIST,

BY

THE AUTHOR.

PREFACE.

I can scarcely tell how I come to write this poem. It was ever my opinion that the Æneid terminated too abruptly, and therefore I thought that a continuation of the history of Æneas would fill a void which the distinguished Latin poet had left. Discarding the fable of the twins and the wolf, I have made Æneas the founder of Rome.

I have thus launched my poetic bark on the public wave, subject to all the storms which the critics may direct against it.

ALEXANDER EVANS.

INTRODUCTION.

The classical reader will remember that the twelfth book of Dryden's translation of Virgil's Æniad closes with the death of Turnus, the Daunian Prince. Where that history ends my story begins. The reader will also remember that King Latinus had an only child, the Princess Lavinia; Turnus was a suitor for her hand, but King Latinus, from the omen of a swarm of bees that settled in his orchard, believed that a foreign Prince was to succeed him on his throne. The contest, therefore, was to be decided by single combat, and the victor was to have the Princess. Æneas was the victor. How successfully the author has kept up the heathen Mythological machinery, the reader must judge. As the author had nothing to translate from, if there be any merit in the incidents related, the generous reader will give him the proper credit.

Anchises died in Sicily before Æneas reached Italy, hence the sending for his remains.

ARGUMENT.

—

After the death of Turnus a battle ensues, in which the Latins are defeated. Æneas offers thanks for his victory —the ceremonies are interrupted by some discontented warriors. They are chided by Venus. Juno vents her wrath. Æneas consults a Sybil, who tells him of the future glories of Rome. A triumphal procession is inaugurated, which the author attempts most elaborately to describe. After various incidents Æneas sends his son Ascanias to Sicily, to obtain the bones of his father, Anchises. He is successful in his mission: returns to Rome with the remains, where they are buried with proper funereal ceremonies, with which the book closes.

ÆNEAS.

Now when the haughty Turnus breathed no more,
His shining armor stained with crimson gore,
The Latins, struck with horror at the sight,
In terror yield, and flee in dread affright;
To haste their speed and urge them on their way,
They gladly threw their burnished shields away,
And golden armor bright as rosy-beaming day;
Dense clouds of dust far o'er the plains arise,
Enshadow friends and shade the lurid skies;
Borne here and there the swift retreating foe
Flies madly on to shun the deadly blow;
Wild shrieks are heard amid the waveless air,
The dying howl loud in their bloody lair;
A crimson carnage stains the grassy plain,
A stream of blood tints Tiber to the main;

Pursuing soldiers clear the battle field,
And hail as victor the Vulcanian shield.

ÆNEAS OFFERS THANKS FOR THE VICTORY.

Soon as the storm, by victory lulled at last,
Has swept its fury o'er the war's wild blast,
The Trojan hero calls his lords around,
And humbly bending on the sacred ground,
His hands uplifted to the smiling skies,
In loud, sonorous accent thus he cries:
"Forever let our thanks, fair goddess, be
Poured out in one eternal stream to thee;
Thou brough'st him safe from Ilion's falling tower,
And crown'st him victor in this happy hour;
For all his toils and dangers of the wave,
Where oft he thought to find an unknown grave,
For troubles past he richly is repaid,
The victory his and his the queenly maid."
He said no more, but caused with watchful care,
An altar built, in form a perfect square.

Some bring the stones the sacred pile to rear;

Around the scene the anxious priests appear,

And with their smiles the laboring workmen cheer;

Some wield the axe to fell the slender pine,

Some round the altar wreaths of flowers entwine,

Here minstrel fingers touch the harp divine;

Triumphant anthems through the ether fly,

A moment charm, then pierce the listening sky,

And far in space in mellow cadence die.

An hundred rams yield holy sacrifice,

A cream-white bullock on the altar dies,

The pleasing incense seeks appoving skies.

THE CEREMONIES ARE INTERRUPTED BY SOME DISCON-TENTED WARRIORS.

Whilst thus the hours in holy rites employ

The priests and lords who came from fallen Troy,

Imploring blessings from the gods above

And offering thanks to Venus, queen of love,

Some veteran warriors round the altar came;

With lips of scorn they mock the sacred flame,

And taunt the mention of great Hector's name.

The patron goddess hears, with saddened soul,

The murmurs which their minds could not control.

" Why give to Hector honor greater far,

Than we have gained through all this Latium war?

He fell untimely on the Trojan plain,

Long months remained among the unburied slain,

Whilst we have braved the dangers of the main,

On fair Italia's fruitful fields have won

Enduring fame for Troy's wandering son."

THEY ARE CHIDED BY VENUS.

" You shame yourselves," the haughty queen replies,

Descending swift from rosy-colored skies,

Her ire aroused and flashing from her eyes.

" Will you upon the god-like Hector's name

Now seek to cast the shadow of a shame?

Around the walls of Troy his noble form,

Faced Grecian arms and braved the battle-storm;

His courage, like the sun, in splendor shone!

His arm the shield to Priam's royal throne,

Proud Ilion's glory and the nation's joy,

The sainted hero of ill-fated Troy."

The queen dissolves in waves of viewless air,

She and her nymphs to heavenly courts repair,

Enough to know from her celestial frown,

They shall not tarnish Hector's great renown,

Nor mock the rites devoted to the name,

Whose deeds in war have blazon'd Trojan fame.

The chided chiefs abashed, with sorrow sigh,

Afraid to meet Æneas' angered eye;

Their hands uplifted to the Prince they wave,

And bowing low his pardon humbly crave;

The generous Prince the pardon freely gave.

CEREMONIES CONTINUED.

Far to the west the sun's bright chariot flies,

And there the god in purple grandeur dies;

The smiling night enrobes the sleeping earth,

And absent Phœbus gives the stars their birth.

With royal feast the chiefs conclude the fete,

Flushed with wild joy, their hearts with hope elate

Of future glory for the new-born state.

The booty taken on the battle field,

Enormous treasures to the Trojans yield,

Rich in war's arms of javelin, sword and shield.

The Prince these trophies gathers from the ground,

And with them builds a monumental mound;

He sends his soldiers searching o'er the plain,

With pious care gives burial to the slain;

Glad songs of joy throughout the camp resound;

The pealing notes float o'er the echoing ground;

The distant hills reverberate the sound;

Their armor doff, their shields aside they lay,

Proud of the triumph of that glorious day;

And when the earth put on her robe of stars,

In peaceful sleep they banish dreadful wars.

JUNO VENTS HER WRATH.

From jewelled throne in violet-blushing sky,

The wrathful Juno saw the Latins fly;

The mournful sight gave to her breast a pang,

Celestial regions with her moanings rang;

Thus to her nymphs, whilst on her throne enshrined,

She vents the griefs that agonize her mind:

" The Trojan hero, smiled upon by Jove,

And basking in the beams of Venus' love,

Vaunts o'er the field elate with victor's joy,

In triumph now forgets his ruined Troy;

A partial fate for his renown prevails,

And Neptune's favor gave him prosperous gales;

O, were I not immortal, I would fly,

Seek out some cavern and contented die;

But fate decrees—I can but now obey,

And mourn the sorrows of this fatal day;

Though here the Trojan shall erect his throne,

And kings, untold, the mighty empire own,

Give birth to heros, bards with lyres divine,

And cluster glories round the Julian line,

Yet will I watch the fabric as it grows,

Wild fortune's wave as through all time it flows,

See the proud city, with its massive wall,
Rise in her might and then in ruins fall."

ÆNEAS CONSULTS A SIBYL.

Now when the king of day his race had run,
And steeds that draw the chariot of the sun,
In gilded stalls their weary forms repose,
Æneas from his couch in silence rose,
Sought the fair Sibyl in the sylvan wood,
Whose temple on the banks of Tiber stood;
The priestess came from eastern lands afar
And cheered the Trojans in their doubtful war,
By Venus' order gave the Prince of Troy
New hopes, new courage, and his fears destroy;
The Prince advances with a martial air,
His noble looks, his heavenly birth declare,
His form and stately mein immortal lineage wear.
"Oh, favored hero," thus the priestess cried,
"You've won the victory and the lovely bride,
Troy and Italia now in union join,
For future bard immortal themes shall coin;

"A grand republic shall in splendor rise

Whose sway shall reach from east to western skies;

Her conquering banners float in every breeze,

Her navy have no rival on the seas;

Eastward to where the sun on Indus smiles,

And westward conquer Britain's anchored isles.

Enough of glory shall thy children know,

To cheer thy spirit in the shades below,

And through each era of all time to come,

Roll the rich glories of eternal Rome."

TRIUMPHAL PROCESSION.

Now when the stars their silver light withdrew,

And morning woke with brow adorned with dew,

Rich sparkling beams from golden orient flew,

And streaming down the blue enamelled skies,

Paint hill and vale with amber-colored dyes,

And brilliant flame from Phœbus' chariot flies,

The Prince on steed of purest blooded bay,

In armor cased salutes the blushing day;

Before him march two hundred of his guard,

With shields of gold, the veteran's proud reward;

Each bears an emblem of the Goddess Fame,

By warlike deeds each won a warior's name,

And purest Trojan lineage proudly claim.

Now twice three score of youths in rich array,

With vests of gold adorn the victor's way,

And with glad songs they celebrate the day.

Twelve virgins clad in robes of purest white

The willing votaries of the vestal light,

With silver wands in graceful order move,

Reflecting homage to the mighty Jove.

Some fifty soldiers representing Fame,

In shining armor, next in order came,

Each bearing vase containing rich perfume,

Etherial fires the precious oils consume.

A silver car with pyramid of shields,

And other arms, the trophies of the fields,

Drawn by a score of milk-white prancing steeds,

By Tinus driven, famed for heroic deeds.

The conquered Latins gazing on this car,

Reminded them their cruel fate in war.

Twelve war-worn soldiers bearing shields of gold,

The zodiac signs their radiant faces hold,

A scene of splendor gorgeous to behold;

The seven stars, Orion's brilliant band,

The Bear and Dipper of celestial land;

A million jewels form the milky way,

And blazing diamonds comets tracks display;

The evening star reflects its light divine,

And Mars and Pallas in bright armor shine;

The myriad worlds beam on each golden shield,

And morning stars their orient flashes yield;

The Spring in bloom and Autumn's chilly plains,

The Summer here, and there the Winter reigns.

Auraclus next, his brows with ivy crowned,

In gilded robes that swept along the ground,

Emblem of Bacchus, god of purple wine,

Of mighty revels and the fruitful vine.

2

Next came Apollo's priest with tuneful lyre,
From which at times he drew Promethean fire,
And praised in verse the deeds of son and sire.
An urn of gold, intended to contain
The sacred ashes of each hero slain,
On antique car, with silver cloth o'erspread,
(The cloth came from Lavinia's virgin bed),
Next in the cavalcade in order stood,
Drawn by twelve steeds of Babylonian blood,
Steeds reared near the Red Sea's crimson flood.
On gilded car some fifteen cubits long,
A burnished galley laid its length along;
A score of youths in golden vestures shine,
And with their oars they cleave the fancied brine;
High on the poop, in sternest grandeur stands
The dauntless pilot, issuing his commands,
And steers his bark to shun engulphing sands;
The captain aft a triple trident bore,
And points the way to Latium's promised shore;

The trident mounted on a golden rod,

Eternal emblem of the sea-born god,

Whose kindly love the Trojan heroes save

From direful storm and anger-foaming wave,

And drawn by steeds that King Latinus gave.

By twelve black steeds in gorgeous harness clad,

A car was drawn, and on its top was laid

A silver cask filled with Italian wine,

Sacred to Bacchus and the generous vine,

The staves with rubies rich in radiance shine;

An hundred Bacchanalians dance along,

Some sound the tymbrel, some rehearse the song,

Their charming notes go quivering through the skies,

And Calliope's band in melody replies.

Divine Alcides fiery chargers drove

To chariot, sacred to the regal Jove;

The god's gold statue graced the gilded car,

And darts through space his lightning shafts afar,

On ideal foe his thunder bolts he hurls,

And seems to shake the universe of worlds;

In fancied thought you see his awful nod,

His royal face displays the mighty god;

Olympus trembles at imperial eyes,

And dreadful thunders roll through yielding skies.

Next in line some fifty virgins came,

Each bearing torches with a ceaseless flame;

Rich golden robes their graceful limbs adorn,

The robes with jewels shine like rosy morn,

When Phœbus in his chariot mounts the sky,

And golden sparks through all the ether fly;

The goddess Venus claims the lovely throng,

And to her praise they chant the sacred song.

Next came a gilded car of curious form,

One side is bathed in sunlight, one in storm;

Celestial orbs their radiant smiles display,

The moon reflects the night, the sun the day,

And there in beauty Venus' temple stood,

Graced by the sibyl of the sylvan wood.

Last in the triumph young Ascanias came,

A Trojan scion of aspiring fame;

ÆNEAS.

The youthful Prince with graceful martial mein,
Is smiled upon by Latium's future queen;
His golden buckler mirrors morning's beam,
Bright as the face of some transparent stream,
Reflects, through far off ages yet to come,
Resplendent glories for imperial Rome.

ÆNEAS DEMANDS LAVINIA AS HIS BRIDE.

And now descending from triumphal car,
The Trojan Prince proud victor in the war,
Resolves at once to claim the promised maid,
And calm the fears of Priam's restless shade;
Two royal ghosts the wandering Trojan meet,
The one at Delos' isle, and one at Crete,
Give him to know his empire was not there,
But further west he should with speed repair;
Seek out the land, Italia's softened skies,
Where fruitful plain in spreading beauty lies,
And Ætna's belchings kiss the bending skies.
Before one moon had lost its borrowed light,
He seeks Latinus' court in armor bright,

Claims from the King Lavinia as his bride,

Of all her sex the glory and the pride.

"Renowned King, some kindly guiding star,

Has made me victor in this cruel war;

No selfish motives have my actions weighed,

Or vile ambition e'er my duty swayed;

By savage war and fallen Troy driven,

And frowned upon by gods, and vengeful heaven,

I launch my galleys on uncertain sea,

Accept the fortune which the fates decree;

The King of Gods, great Jove himself demands,

To build new Troy in far off western lands;

In fair Lavinia and myself behold

The Roman glories by the bards foretold."

The Prince was silent; then the King began,

"Oh, Trojan Prince, oh, more than mortal man,

Some awful doom, some high decree of fate,

Points you to rule the future Latin state,

Give you the fair Lavinia as your bride,

Our queenly daughter and our regal pride;

Your nuptials now our royal thoughts engage,

No longer wars in direful vengeance rage,

But far above each hero's silent grave,

The hours of peace their olive branches wave;

The maid I yield, your valor's proud reward,

Her virgin honor and her safety guard."

NUPTIAL CEREMONIES.

The golden sun with smiling beams adorn

The dew-bathed brow of soft awakening morn;

The chariot whirling through the ambient skies,

In gilded splendor fair Aurora flies,

And bathes the earth in floods of amber-dyes.

An hundred Lords in gilded vests arrayed,

Escort the Prince to wed the queenly maid;

Some fifty youths their brows with ivy twine

With tuneful fingers touch the lyre divine,

Proclaim the graces of the royal bride,

The queen of beauty and her father's pride,

Latinus, drawn by steeds of creamy white,

In Golden chariot dazzling to the sight;

Himself in diamond-jetted robe arrayed,

Precedes the chariot of the queenly maid,

In stylish and in royal splendor move,

To altar sacred to the god of love;

Where at the temple holy priests preside,

In flowing robes await the coming bride;

All wear a face of brightly beaming joy,

Smile on the maid and greet the Prince of Troy,

Around the altar lamps of incense burn,

And richest perfumes fill each golden urn;

In sculptured marble Venus there presides,

Of love the goddess and of youthful brides;

There Jupiter the god of awful thunder,

Whom heaven hath joined let no man put asunder,

But true to vows pledged on the bridal day,

Seek not from holy nuptial couch to stray;

The priest declares the Prince and Princess one,

The rites performed the pleasing task is done,

The Prince a bride and glorious kingdom won.

Two silver moons with shields of silver light,

Sacred alone to awe-inspiring night,

Into the misty past had winged their flight

Before the royal games had ceased to charm,

And mimic battle scenes no longer warm

The public heart; rejoicings all have fled

And silence reigns as with the buried dead;

The wars are o'er, the bride and kingdom won

And fame with laurels crowns proud Ilion's son;

The Latin lords, who late with Turnus fought,

With humble mein the courtly presence sought;

Lucanian heroes and the Daunian brave,

Rutulian nobles all their homage gave,

And flags of peace alone in beauty wave.

No clouds of war disturb the beaming sky,

No mail-clad soldiers on their coursers fly.

But smiling peace in gentle sweetness reigns,

And ample harvests gild the waving plains;

The shepherds under spreading shades recline,

Attend their flocks and prune luxuriant vine,

And press from grapes the rich Italian wine;

The matrons at their looms, now weave and sing,

The maids the water bear from crystal spring,

At close of day the artless, happy throng,

On moon-lit lawn begin the dance and song;

The nightingale enchants with soft delight

And glow worms add their sparkles to the night;

The teeming earth puts forth her richest flowers,

And shepherd swains make love in floral bowers;

Now god of war has ceased his bloody reign,

And gentle peace reposes o'er the plain.

VARIOUS INCIDENTS.

Revolving suns spring's genial course had run,

And fruitful summer had her task begun;

Now weary with a life of idle joy,

The Prince reflects upon his ruined Troy,

Remembers what the iron fates demand,

To build new Ilion on Italian land,

And there in splendor let new glories rise,

And waft her hero's fame to future skies,

Through ages roll the royal Trojan name,

Each era adding to its glorious fame,

The Prince is chided in a dream at night,

By old Anchises' ghost in armor bright;

"Why thus, my son," he said, "supinely lay,

In slothful ease consume each fleeting day?

Shall Priam's ghost on ruined Troy's shore,

His hapless fate for endless time deplore?

No peaceful tomb receive his sacred form,

Shall he be left to brave earth's bitter storm?

For shame, my son, forsake your couch of ease,

And Priam's shade and my sad ghost appease."

Like storm-tossed bark upon some troubled stream,

The Prince awakened from his ghostly dream,

He seeks the Sibyl in the shady wood,

Where Tiber rolls her yellow colored flood;

There in the temple sacred to some god,

The priestess wields a silver pointed rod;

Greets kings and heros clad in mail of gold,

And in prophetic words their fates unfold:

" Again I come to learn my future fate,

Where build the city of the new-born state;

If sparkling glories shall reward my toil,

Or desolating war my days embroil;

What joys or sorrows are reserved for me,

What is the gods and stubborn fates decree?"

Long silence reigned; the priestess now behold

In trembling state, as pierced by chilling cold

In wildest phrenzy rolls her glancing eyes,

Now scans the earth and now prophetic skies;

On brazen altar sweetest incense burns,

And magic charms are held in shining urns;

" Now where the Tiber's waters kiss the sea,

There build the town; it is the fates decree;

Nor further seek your destiny to know,

Whether of glory or of anguished woe;

Enough of grandeur cluster round thy name

To weave a webb inlaced with glorious fame."

Bright as the golden sun's first sparkling beam,

That wanders west to kiss the gliding stream,

The Prince revolves the Sibyl's wonderous dream;

He calls a council of his Trojan band,

On neighing steed goes forth to view the land;

Where Tiber's waters rocky inlets lave,

And seven hills o'erlook the frowning wave;

He there decides to build the future town,

There let the fates unfold his great renown,

And like the fires that in wild forests rise,

Shoot forth their flames, illumine all the skies.

The fame of heroes yet unborn shall blaze,

And with their deeds a startled world amaze.

Propitious offering to the gods are made,

And prayers to rest Anchises' wandering shade;

The friendly sea-nymphs dwellers in the wave,

Receive adorings from the Trojan brave;

To Neptune, ocean's god, they bow the knee,

To him give glory in a high degree,

And his attendant train, the daughters of the sea.

A score of bullocks furnish sacrifice

To Jupiter, the thunderer of the skies;

The entrails point to deeds of future fame,
That time to come will clothe the Trojan name,
Bear Rome's proud banner through a host of wars,
And conquered kings chain to triumphal cars.
Here lines are drawn, and trenches broad and deep
In crescent form, around the city sweep;
The ramparts here, and there the towers arise,
The earth their base, their tops salute the skies;
Some builders came from far Phœnician shore,
And some from Egypt lent their skillful lore;
In distinct bands the various trades are classed
Some hew the stones, some rocky quarries blast;
These fell the trees to clear the sacred ground,
The echoing music from the hills rebound;
A palace here and stately columns rise,
And there a temple greets approving eyes;
On every hill a stately dome is seen,
Whilst troubled Tiber rolls his waves between,
Long years glide by, the walls in grandeur rise,
And altars waft their incense to the skies;

An infant state adores its guiding star,

And cultivates the arts of peace and war;

Here the proud Trojan makes his second home,

And Troy again lives in imperial Rome.

The thought that old Anchisis' dust remains,

Uneasy rests on fair Sicilia's plains;

His wandering ghost in sadness roams around,

No resting place, no sacred tomb has found,

Destroys the peace Æneas might have known,

And poisons half the pleasures of his throne;

His mind disturbed by torturing dreams at night,

And day but brings the tombless shade to light.

The queen Lavinia marks with anguished care,

His soul is shadowed by some wild despair;

Some unknown grief is gnawing at his breast,

Destroys his peace and poisons all his rest.

"What grieves my lord," whilst tears bedim her eyes,

Her bosom heaving with sad-speaking sighs;

"Tell me, the partner of your joys and woes,

To me your secret sorrows all disclose;

Let me but know what racks your kingly mind,

What aching misery in your breast confined:

The troubled shadows from your soul dispel,

Nor let them there one moment longer dwell."

Æneas to the queen his thoughts disclose,

Unveils to her the secret of his woes;

The restless state of Priam's wandering shade,

Anchises' bones so long from tomb delayed;

The first left on the smoking Trojan plain,

On rights neglected casts a high disdain;

The last, unburied, roams Sicilia's fair domain.

These deep regrets consume Æneas' mind,

Like galleys blown by Boreas' treacherous wind.

At last great Jove his tortured mind resolves,

And troublous sorrow into joy dissolves.

Then to Ascanias, thus the father cries,

Whilst beaming pleasure sparkles in his eyes:

"Go, man your fleet and risk the angry tide,

To fair Sicilia's shore in safety ride;

Acestes still in regal splendor reigns,

There old Anchises' hallowed dust remains;

Seek out the place where rests his sacred form;

Your ships shall baffle waves and tropic storm;

Bring forth the bones we left in foreign land—

Haste to obey your loving sire's command."

The freighted galleys leave the Latin shore,

Strong arms with vigor wield the bending oar,

The waves around in angry hoarseness roar.

Now o'er the waters, through the foaming tide,

The galleys shoot and storms in safety ride;

The sun their guide when day was clear and bright,

The moon and stars direct their course at night;

The ocean king provides the favoring breeze,

And sea nymphs press the galleys through the seas.

Now direful storms envelope sea and sky,

Terrific gales through blackened ether fly;

Loud claps of thunder through the air resound,

The tossing vessels tremble at the sound.

3

The lightning's flash lights up the stormy clouds,

As if to show the crews their future shrouds;

But firm to duty every seaman stood,

And with strong arms they brave the raging flood,

Meantime the ruler of the watery realm,

Preserves the vessels and directs each helm;

Safe through the storm the reeling barks he guides,

Unharmed o'er waves each galley proudly rides,

Colossus-like each billowy hill bestrides.

The consort-queen had prayed the mighty Jove,

To send the storm and lighting from above,

To sink the Trojan fleet beneath the wave,

And give to every soul a tombless grave:

The awful god yields to his queen's desire,

And from Olympus darts his fearful fire,

Hurls forth his thunders from celestial throne,

(This power belongs to Jupiter alone,)

Enveils the skies with clouds of deepest black,

And blinds the pilots in their watery track.

But Jove well knew that Neptune's watchful care,
Would guard the vessels from each dangerous snare,
And send them safely to their destined home,
Through wild, high rolling waves and maddened foam,
The queen, thus foiled, beholds with tearful eye,
The clouds disperse and smiles cerulean sky;
Far on its way the fleet in safety sails
Bright skies above and fanned by wooing gales,
Till anchored fast in calm Sicilian bay,
The storm-tossed barks in peaceful harbor lay,
And thankful hearts all hail the glorious day.
Scarce had the sun with silver beams of light,
Adorned day's brow and chased away the night,
When young Ascanias rose from balmy sleep,
And offers thanks to guardians of the deep;
Safe through the storm, and through the surging main,
The Trojan barks the friendly harbor gain;
A snow white dove on hissing altar burns;
And charming incense smokes in brazen urns;

A spotless ram upon the altar lies,
And fervent prayer ascends to sacred skies;
The far off sky, home of imperial Jove,
And Venus, goddess of unchanging love.
Now when Ascanias had an ending made,
In pleasing prayers invoked Anchises' shade,
He sees from far a golden-bannered train,
In gilded armor marching o'er the plain;
Down to the beach the brilliant cavalcade,
Descend in order, 'neath the laurel shade;
And thus Eutolus, captain of the band,
Gives Prince Ascanias welcome to the land.
" Acestes, who from royal Trojan flood
Bears in his veins proud Ilion's noble blood,
Bids me give welcome to the youthful lord,
And ask the fates his prowess to reward:
Why have you sought Sicilia's fertile land,
What is your wish, your Kingly sire's command?"
Then thus Ascanias: " Know our arms have won
The Latin realm; our warfare now is done;

But still Anchises' sacred bones remain,

Within Sicilia's fair and loved domain;

These prized and hallowed relics I require,

To calm the shade of great Æneas' sire."

When King Acestes learned that Trojans came

Anchises' bones and lifeless dust to claim;

From ivory throne, in royal, golden chair,

Fanned by Arabia's perfumed ladened air,

He bids Ascanias welcome to his land,

In person asks to know his sire's command.

Again Ascanias, in Æneas' name,

Told King Acestes of his modest claim;

His only wish the hallowed shade shall rest·

In Rome's imperial and eternal breast.

"Thou glorious youth, born of a race divine,

And doomed to grace the distant Julian line,

Bear Roman arms through years of crimson war

And fame unending roll in time's swift car;

The lost you seek, the lost shall yet be found

If yet that lost remains within our ground;

The gods themselves, shall further your design
And fates their mandates to your wish resign."
The royal monarch gave his lords command,
To see the crews were safely housed on land;
In rich abundance furnish daily food,
For those who had the waves and storms withstood;
All, at his hands receive a welcome warm—
He seeks alone their weary hearts to charm.
In his own palace young Ascanias dwelt,
And all a monarch's kindness daily felt.
Three days had sunk beneath the waves of time,
Three nights were passed in mild Sicilian clime,
The fourth beheld the sun, with golden brow,
From orient rise; the priests in temples bow,
And offer up to Mars and mighty Jove
The sacrifice of mortal's hallowed love;
To brave Ascanias give a favoring smile,
Crown with success his visit to their isle;
Return him safe to Latium's sacred land,
With watchful favor guard his Trojan band.

Two hundred horsemen clad in mail of steel,

Their radiant shields the zodiac signs reveal,

In martial order seek the hallowed grove,

Where tombs arise and restless spirits rove;

There 'neath the shade of blooming laurel trees,

Above the sleeping sighs the mournful breeze;

There in the bosom of a grassy mound,

The great Anchises' sacred bones are found:

The aged Sicilian monarch, wise and just,

To golden urn transfers the pious dust,

And in the hands of young Ascanias gave,

The sad remains of Troy's honored brave.

The barks are manned, the whitened sails are spread,

And crews embark without a fear or dread;

Bright silver beams flash through the radiant sky,

Illume the waves and through the ether fly;

The troubled seas the barks in safety bear,

And by their sides with ever watchful care,

Anchises' shade glides through the yielding air;

The buoyant galleys cleave the briny tide,

In graceful style the playing wavelets ride;

Before their bows the sea nymphs part the foam,

And waft them safely to their destined home.

Meantime Æneas, moved by pious love,

Prepared a tomb within a shady grove,

With anxious thoughts awaits the coming day,

The fleet shall plow the waters of the bay,

And safe at anchor in the harbor lay.

Time presses on, the sunny hours fly,

And Luna's chariot rolls amid the sky.

The flying moments bring the fleet at last,

Through angry waves and Boreas' howling blast;

No soul is gone, no vessel lost an oar,

The fleet, unharmed, returns to Latium's shore.

A thousand lords in gilded armor shine,

A hundred banners sparkle down the line,

In solemn but in martial order move

To temple sacred to imperial Jove;

On burnished altar bleeding offerings burn,

And priests in robes receive the sacred urn;

Ascanias now resigns his weighty trust

By yielding up Anchises' hallowed dust;

The priest received the treasure from his hand,

And whilst he spoke he waved a golden wand:

"Oh, brave Ascanias, may the mighty god

Who shakes Olympus with his awful nod;

May Jupiter whose dreadful thunders roll

From sky to earth and awe the human soul;

May all the gods their richest favors yield,

And stamp thy glories on thy golden shield;

To future ages blazon thy renown,

And with eternal fame thy temples crown;

The sea-born god the favoring breezes gave,

Preserved thy galleys from the treacherous wave;

And now in marble dome the shade shall rest,

And smile in peace among the sainted blest;

No care, no toil shall e'er his shadow know

But dwell in glory with the shades below."

The costly incense yields a perfumed flame,

The holy rites the Trojans' homage claim,

And shrine with love Anchises' honored name.

Æneas placed the urn in marble vault,

His sire's renown and virtuous deeds exalt;

" Thou hallowed shade and sad remains of Troy,

Unending life of fame and love enjoy;

A coronet of virtues crown thy brow,

And at thy shrine thy latest lineage bow;

Let heroes, yet to come, revere thy name,

And monarchs seek to rival thy bright fame;

Eternal glory welcome thee above,

Thou who hast won the gods' and mortals' love;

To earth, thy mother, we consign thy dust,

The good, the true, the ever brave and just;

Roam there in peace in blest Elysian fields,

Where Venus reigns and Jove his sceptre wields;

No time shall dim or rolling ages fade

The honored name thy virtuous deeds have made;

But years eternal shall thy glory shrine,

And wreaths of love around thy memory twine."

A solemn silence charms the listening ear,

Approving smiles in cloudless skies appear;

The wandering winds through waving leaflets sigh,

The saddened cadence lingers in the sky,

Till faint with breath in distant regions die;

The classic grove that waves its leafy head,

Joins in the dirge around the sleeping dead;

The virgins, vestals of the ceaseless light,

With wood-nymphs guard the sacred tomb at night;

The air-sprites chant a dirge above the grave,

And Tiber's waters swell the music wave;

In sculptured tomb of Parian marble made,

By pious hands the lifeless dust is laid,

And thus in glory sleeps the royal Trojan's shade.